This book belongs to

⋯⋯⋯⋯⋯⋯⋯⋯⋯⋯⋯⋯⋯⋯⋯⋯⋯

⋯⋯⋯⋯⋯⋯⋯⋯⋯⋯⋯⋯⋯⋯⋯⋯⋯

To the Castle

To Beyond

Written and illustrated by
Steve Smallman

First published by Parragon in 2008

Parragon
Queen Street House
4 Queen Street
Bath BA1 1HE, UK

ISBN 978-1-4075-1288-4
Printed in China

Little Dragon

Makes Friends

Bath · New York · Singapore · Hong Kong · Cologne · Delhi · Melbourne

Little Dragon is reading a book all about a nasty man in a tin suit who bashes up poor little dragons.

Little Dragon feels all worried and shaky.

Just then, Little Dragon hears voices outside.
"Oh, no!" thinks Little Dragon. "Dragon-bashers!"
And he hides under his blanket.

Outside, Princess Pippa, Prince Pip, and Little Baron Boris are walking up the hill. Boris is making a lot of noise and waving a wooden sword around his head.

"Let's go on a dragon hunt," says Boris. "Are you coming?"

"No thank you," say Pippa and Pip.

"Scaredy cats, scaredy cats!" sings Boris.

"We are **not** scaredy cats!" says Pip angrily.

"Let's go then!" says Boris smugly.

"Look!" cries Boris. "Dragon footprints!"

They follow the footprints right up to Little Dragon's door.

"Er ... you two go first," says Boris, "I'll stand outside and guard the door in case the dragon tries to escape."

Pip and Pippa push the door open and creep inside.

It's **very** dark and spooky inside the cave.
They see a light coming toward them, and
a big shadow that looks like ...

a dragon!

They are very frightened!

"Who's there?" asks Pip bravely.
"It's me!" says Little Dragon.
"Who's me?" asks Pip.
"I am," says Little Dragon.

"Are you a real dragon?"
asks Pippa.

"Yes, I'm Little Dragon,"
says Little Dragon.
"You're very small," says Pippa.
"I'm big on the inside," says Little Dragon,
standing on tippy toes to make himself look taller.

Then Little Dragon starts to cry.

"Are you going to bash me up now, like in my book?" he sniffs.

"We don't want to bash you," says Princess Pippa.

"Not even a little bit?" asks Little Dragon.

"Of course not!" says Pippa, and she gives him a big hug.

"Let's just be friends instead," says Prince Pip.

So that is settled.

"Would you like some tea?" asks Little Dragon.
"Oh, yes please!" say Pippa and Pip.
They sit down on a rug and Little Dragon fetches
them big plates of cupcakes and sandwiches.

"Yummy, yummy for my tummy!" says Pip and takes a big bite of jelly sandwich. All the jelly squirts out and everybody laughs.

"Does your friend want a cupcake?" asks Little Dragon.

"What friend?" asks Pippa.

"The noisy one with the pointy stick," says Little Dragon.

"Oh, you mean Boris," says Pippa. "I'm sure he'd like a cake, he's always hungry!"

"Hello!" says Little Dragon.

"It's a dragon!" cries Little Baron Boris.
Then he runs away as fast as he can.
"Now who's a scaredy cat?" says Pip, laughing.

Soon it is time for Pip and Pippa to go home.

"Please can we be friends tomorrow too?" asks Little Dragon.

"Not just tomorrow," say Pip and Pippa, "we'll be friends for ever and ever!"

Yippee!

"Yippee!" shouts Little Dragon, "I like friends!"

The End

Now that you have read the story, join in the fun!

(almost)

Look carefully at the pictures,
then answer the questions:

Who is eating a
jelly sandwich?

What color is
Princess Pippa's drink?

How many cupcakes can you count?